STO

FRIENDS
OF ACPL

PETE'S PUP

3 Puppy Stories by Syd <u>Hoff</u>

Windmill Books, Inc. and E. P. Dutton & Co., Inc.

New York

Text and illustrations copyright © 1975 by Syd Hoff
Published by Windmill Books & E. P. Dutton & Co.
201 Park Avenue South, New York, New York 10003

Library of Congress Cataloging in Publication Data
Hoff, Sydney   Pete's pup
SUMMARY: Three stories about Pete's tiny new
puppy, its tremendous growth, and the unusual pet it
acquires out of loneliness.
[1. Dogs—Fiction.   2. Pets—Fiction]   I. Title.
PZ7.H672Pg   [E]   74-26718   ISBN 0-525-61507-5

Published simultaneously in Canada by Clarke,
Irwin & Company, Limited, Toronto and Vancouver
Printed in the U.S.A.   First Edition
10 9 8 7 6 5 4 3 2 1

Pete's parents got him a pup.
He was so small,
he fit right in Pete's hand.

"Would you have wanted
a bigger pup?" asked
Pete's mother and father.

"No, thanks,
I only want this one,"
said Pete.

Pete put his pup on the rug.

He almost got lost in the pile.

Pete put his pup on the sofa.

He almost disappeared
between two pillows.

Pete brought his pup a little
bowl of water to drink.

Pete's pup fell into the bowl
and **Pete** had to pull him
out before he drowned.

"Take him outside and
see that he gets some fresh air.
Maybe that way he'll grow,"
said Pete's parents.

Pete took his pup
out on the lawn.

The gardener almost ran over
him with the mower.

Pete put his pup on the sidewalk.

A lady passing by
almost stepped on him.

"Oh, well, I guess I'll just
have to hold on to you,"
said Pete, and he kept his pup
in his arms all afternoon.

Pete's friends started
to play ball. "Maybe I could
have just one catch,"
thought Pete, putting his
pup down on the ground.

Pete caught one ball,
and another,
and still another....

The game was over.
"Where's my pup?" asked Pete.

"There he is down the street,
going in the gutter!"
shouted his friends.

Pete ran to the corner
and grabbed his pup
just in time!

"I'm sorry that I'm so small
and cause so much trouble.
What will happen if I don't grow?
How will I be able
to make you like me?"
Pete's pup seemed to ask.

"Just be my pup," said Pete,
holding him close, and he
knew he would never take his
eyes off his pup again, and
would love him forever and ever.
No matter how big or small he
was, he was just right for Pete.

PUP CARE TIPS

1. Pup should be six to eight weeks old when you bring him home.

2. Bring pup home in the daytime.

3. Pup's quarters should be ready.

4. Make pup's bed from a wire cage or a wooden box with high sides.

5. Place a flat, washable cushion or an old, folded blanket at one end of the bed and some newspaper at the other end.

6. Keep pup's bed in one place so he will always know where "home" is.

7. If pup is nervous, pet him and talk softly to him; he will soon feel better.

8. Don't get pup a collar yet—he will soon grow out of it.

9. Give pup some warm milk just before bedtime.

10. Place a ticking alarm clock and a hot water bottle wrapped in a towel into the bed with your pup to comfort him.

PETE'S PUP'S PET

Pete loved his pup.
"Oh, it's great to have a pet,"
he said, and played with
him all day long.

One day Pete had to go to
school and leave his pup alone.
"I wish I had a pet
of my own," said Pete's pup.

Pete's pup went all over
the house looking for
such a thing.

"Will you be my pet?"
he asked the cat,
bringing her a saucer of milk.

The cat lapped up
all of the milk and
walked away.

"Will you be my pet?"
Pete's pup asked the parakeet,
holding him on his paw
and teaching him to bark.

"Bow-wow," said the parakeet,
and flew back into his cage.

"Oh, dear, who will be
my pet now?" asked Pete's pup,
scratching himself.

A tiny flea
hopped onto the floor!

"Hello," said the flea.
"I'm Freddy, the trained flea."

"Good! Entertain me,"
said Pete's pup,
sitting back to enjoy the show.

Freddy the flea
got down on one knee
and sang a song.

He did a very clever
tap dance.

He stood on his head and
wiggled his ears.

"More! More!" shouted Pete's pup, clapping his paws.

"And now, if you will fetch an
ordinary sewing needle, I
will perform the most difficult
trick of all, a trick no other
flea in the world can do," said
Freddy the flea, taking a bow.

Pete's pup found a needle.
He held it up.
Freddy jumped straight through
the eye of the needle —
blindfolded!

"Oh, you're a wonderful flea!
Please stay and
be my pet," said Pete's pup.

"I'm sorry, but a trained flea belongs in a circus and that's exactly where I'm heading right now," said Freddy. "Anyway, just between you and me, a dog is better off *without* fleas. Goodbye."

He hopped out of the window,
onto another dog that was passing.
"Well, I'm off to the circus!"
"Come see me sometime," he cried.

Pete's pup felt very sad
seeing him go. Just then,
Pete came home from school.
"Hi, pup, let's go out and play."

"Bow-wow," said Pete's pup.
All at once he was perfectly
happy being Pete's pet,
because that's what
a pup is intended to be.

PUP CARE TIPS

1. Start housebreaking your pup at eight to ten weeks of age.

2. When paper training, spread newspaper in a corner spot just for pup.

3. Be sure to spread paper thickly over a wide area.

4. Take pup to his corner right after he has eaten and stay with him.

5. Praise pup highly after he goes on the paper; if he makes a mistake, scold him sharply and carry him over to his paper.

6. Outdoor training means at least two walks each day.

7. Your pup will soon find a favorite outdoor spot.

8. After pup has done his business outside, return home immediately so he will know what the walk was for.

9. When pup has done his business outdoors, praise him highly.

10. At this same age, teach pup to "come," "sit," and "fetch."

PETE'S
PUP GROWS UP

It was fun having a pup.
Every day Pete put him on a leash
and took him for a walk.

"What a nice little pup,"
people said.
"How cute! How nice!"

They stopped to pet Pete's pup.
They scratched him behind
the ears. Pete was very proud.

Then all of a sudden,
Pete's pup started to grow.

He got bigger—

AND BIGGER!

Pete couldn't pull him.
He was pulling *Pete!*

Bumpety-bump! Flippety-flop!
Down the street went Pete,
head over heels, trying to
hold onto the leash!

Pete's pup couldn't fit
in the dog house any more.

He could hardly even fit
in *Pete's* house!

Pete's pup enjoyed his
meal very much.

He enjoyed everyone
else's meal, too!

After dinner the whole family
went into the living room
to watch TV.

They couldn't see a show
because Pete's pup
was in the way!

Pete's father tried
to pick up Pete's pup.
"I'll take you outside."

But Pete's pup
picked *him* up instead!

"Something will have to be done about your pet," said Pete's father. "He's much too big."

Pete's pup tried going on a diet.

He tried doing exercise.

He even tried staying
in a steam room.

It was no use.
He was bigger than ever!

"I know what we have to do,"
said Pete. "We'll just
have to give him lots and lots
of love because there's
so much of him."
And that's what they did.

PUP CARE TIPS

1. Always give your pup plenty of fresh water.

2. Give pup sturdy toys to chew on to strengthen his teeth.

3. Don't feed pup chicken or fish bones.

4. Don't feed your pup scraps at the table.

5. Don't give your pup spicy foods or sweets.

6. Give your pup a good steak bone once in a while.

7. Get your pup a license and a name tag.

8. Give pup a bath about once a month.

9. Take pup to the vet for the shots every pup should have.

10. Let your pup know you love him.